MW00886221

Ricky and the Grim Wrapper

Written by

Allen L. Pier

Illustrated by

James Koenig

Ricky and the Grim Wrapper - story and illustrations by Allen L. Pier

© 2019 Allen L. Pier

All rights reserved. No part of this publication may be reproduced, distributed, or transmitted in any form or by any means, including photocopying, recording, or other electronic or mechanical methods, without the prior written permission of the author, except in the case of brief quotations embodied in critical reviews and certain other noncommercial uses permitted by copyright law. For permission requests, contact the author at rickgrim0611@yahoo.com with the word "Permission" in the subject line.

This book is dedicated
to my wife, Libby, my son, James,
and to his former first grade teacher,
Ms. Presslak, for encouraging me
to publish.

Special thanks to:
My nieces, Mary and Elizabeth,
for engaging young readers,
and providing invaluable feedback.

ALLEN L. PIER

1

1. Ricky's Troublesome Habits

Ricky took one last big bite of his Koko Kid chocolate bar. He crumpled the empty paper wrapper into a tight ball and threw it into the wind as high as he could throw it. The wind grabbed the crumpled wrapper and carried it off in an instant, and Ricky watched with excitement as the little wad of paper danced and swirled, coming to rest on the sidewalk ahead of him, then rolling off into the grass.

Ricky was a good boy, but he had two very troublesome habits. Not only did he not RECYCLE anything, he was a LITTERBUG, too. His mother told him time and again that littering spoiled the otherwise scenic streets, parks and roadsides of their town. She told him that littering was wasteful — that many candy wrappers, lunch bags, milk cartons, and soda pop cans could be recycled. Ricky's father told him that littering was "just plain nasty." But Ricky continued to litter. He threw candy wrappers on the sidewalk, paper drink cups on the street, soda pop cans in the grass, and bubble gum wrappers on the playground. No one could explain why, but wherever Ricky went, he littered. Even Ricky himself could not explain why he littered.

Kiara, Andrew, and Keenan were Ricky's best friends in the whole wide world. They were all Junior Raccoons, and their Raccoon Platoon helped to pick up the litter and garbage that collected along Green Briar Road. Green Briar was the road that ran through town and out into the country, and was Ricky's parents' favorite road for weekend drives. Kiara, Andrew, and Keenan would go out on Saturday afternoons with other Junior Raccoons in their Raccoon Platoon and pick up wrappers, cans, bottles and bags that careless people like Ricky had thrown out into the grass next to the road. Ricky was not the only person in town who littered.

One day Kiara saw Ricky on the playground near their school. She told him he should stop littering, and asked him to help them pick up the trash along Green Briar Road. She, Andrew and Keenan would be going out again on the coming Saturday. Ricky just shrugged his shoulders and walked away. On his way home, he threw another candy wrapper on the sidewalk.

3

2. A MUNCHIN' MIKE'S PICNIC LUNCH

Saturday came, and it was a beautiful sunny day. It was such a perfect day that Ricky's mother suggested they all go for a ride in the country. She said that she would drive, since Ricky's father drove on their last outing. On the way out of town, they stopped for a take-out lunch at their favorite drive-in snack shop, Munchin' Mike's. Ricky loved the food at Munchin' Mike's, and as they drove off down Green Briar Road, the wonderful smells of freshly cooked hamburgers, French fries and onion rings filled the inside of the car. They drove a short way along Green Briar Road and finally pulled off into a peaceful wayside park with a picnic table surrounded by trees. Ricky could hardly wait as they all climbed from the car and sat down to eat their lunch and enjoy the beautiful day.

Ricky had a big, juicy hamburger with French fries and a giant frosty root beer to drink. When they had all finished eating, Ricky's father picked up all the empty wrappers, bags and paper cups. He even picked up a cup someone else had thrown on the ground near their picnic table. Ricky watched as his father carried all the trash over to a nearby trash barrel and threw it all in.

Ricky had not finished his root beer, so he asked his mother if he could take it along in the car. "Okay," she replied, "but remember to save your empty cup until we get home so you can throw it in the trash can behind the garage." Ricky promised to obey his mother's request, and he climbed into the back seat of the family car, happily sipping his root beer.

Ricky's mother slid into the driver's seat and fastened her seat belt. After throwing away all the trash he had collected, Ricky's father walked back to the car, then paused, taking a long, deep breath of the fresh summer air before getting into the car and taking his place in the front passenger's seat. He turned to Ricky's mother and said, "You know, it's such a beautiful day, why don't we take the long way home? We could head north on Green Briar up to the Apple River turn-off. I haven't been out that way in months." They all agreed that would be a wonderful idea, and as Ricky's mother snapped her seatbelt closed, she looked into the rearview mirror, reminding Ricky to fasten his seatbelt, too.

His mother carefully pulled out onto Green Briar Road, turning north instead of south toward home. As they drove along the beautiful country road, Ricky sipped and slurped until the root beer cup was empty except for the ice. The car sped along as his parents chatted happily in the front seat. The wind whistled through the open windows, and the air smelled of fresh-cut grass, flowers and sunshine. Ricky gazed at the clean green roadside as it flowed past the car like a river of grass.

After a few minutes, Ricky and his parents saw a group of Junior Raccoons walking along Green Briar Road with large trash bags. Ricky recognized Kiara, Andrew and Keenan immediately, and he waved excitedly to his friends as they sped past.

"That was Kiara, Andrew and Keenan, wasn't it?" asked Ricky's mother. She looked at Ricky in the rearview mirror and smiled. "Would you be interested in joining Junior Raccoons? Those girls and boys participate in so many wonderful projects, like picking up the litter along Green Briar Road."

Ricky just shrugged and continued sipping his root beer. The cup was now nearly empty. As they travelled on, Ricky's parents eventually stopped talking and began to look out at the passing scenery. Their faces turned from smiling to sad at what they saw as they drove on. Litter of all kinds dotted the green grass that lined Green Briar Road. Cans, cups, bags, and many different candy and gum wrappers had been thrown there by countless careless people. Ricky's mother broke the silence. "I can't believe how little respect people have for our lovely roadside… our town… our planet!"

"But the Junior Raccoons will come and clean it up, Mom!" said Ricky. "They just haven't gotten this far yet."

"Well, that may be true," said his father. "But that won't stop people from littering." Then Ricky's mother added, "Those litterbugs need to be taught a lesson. But how?" No one spoke, and inside the car became so quiet that all that Ricky could hear was the fluttering sound of the wind passing through his open window.

3. THE BIG WHOOSH

After a short while, Ricky felt that funny, edgy feeling that always came over him when he had the urge to litter. Sure, his mother was right that littering is wrong and hurts Mother Nature's feelings, and sure he had promised her that he would save the empty cup for the trash can behind the garage. But those thoughts began to fade as his urge to see the Munchin' Mikes root beer cup dance and swirl in the wind became stronger and stronger. And besides, Kiara, Andrew, Keenan and the other Junior Raccoons would be along to pick up the trash anyway.

In a burst of mischievous energy, Ricky threw the empty root beer cup through the open car window. He looked back excitedly to watch the cup as the wind grabbed it, spinning it toward the parkway that was already spoiled by every kind of litter that one could imagine.

He laughed out loud as the cup began to fall, dancing and whirling toward the ground. His whole body vibrated with an inexplicable electricity that settled over him like a mysterious cloak every time he littered.

But something very strange happened just before the cup hit the roadside. Ricky felt a sudden, almost deafening "WHOOSH!", and he was surrounded by a flash of very bright light. It was brighter than the brightest sunlight he had ever seen. Then he felt as if he were riding on a roller coaster made of wind, somersaulting over and over, and finally landing with a hollow "KWOK."

Ricky lay still for a moment, not knowing what had happened. He was no longer in the car, but was sitting in some very tall grass. How on Earth had he gotten here? "What's going on?" he thought. "Where am I? What happened to me?!"

Now he felt afraid.

Where were his mother and father? Where was the car? Ricky looked around anxiously.

He found it very hard to turn his head. He heard a crackling sound coming from the top of his head as he tried to look around. Ricky turned his head again, and again there was the odd crackling sound. This time he smelled root beer. How strange! He slowly reached up to touch the top of his head.

The top of his head was flat! When he pressed down, there was that crackling noise yet again. He felt around on top of his flat head. There was something sticking up out of his flat, crackling head. It felt like a big, long plastic tube. It felt like a giant straw!

Ricky's heart pounded. "It *IS* a giant straw!" he cried. "And my head is a plastic top!" He couldn't believe what had happened. He thought he must be having a bad dream, but he couldn't wake up!
Now Ricky had to face the weird and frightening truth. *He had turned into the empty root beer cup that he had thrown out the car window!* "How did this happen!?" he blurted.

4. Unknown Voices

Ricky was so afraid he began to cry. "What am I going to do?" he sobbed. "Mommy, where are you? Daddy, where are you? I want to go home! Please, somebody wake me up and take me home!" As his crying slowly turned to a whimper, he could hear something moving in the thick, tall grass. He heard faint voices, too. Maybe his parents heard his cries! Maybe they were coming back to find him! He felt excited and hopeful. The sounds and voices must be his mother and father! "This has to be just a bad dream," he thought.

As the two voices gradually grew louder, Ricky knew they were not his mother's and father's. He did not recognize them at all. He tried to move lower into the grass, hoping he would not be seen by the approaching strangers. The two voices became clearer as the strangers approached. The first was very deep and rough, and sounded angry. "Look, kid" the voice said, "You're new. You have high hopes. I've been on this roadside for a long time. Believe me, once you wind up here, you'll be here forever!"

"Gee, Mr. Rusty," replied the second voice, "I'm not a tin can like you. I'm aluminum!" This voice was a young girl's voice and reminded Ricky of Kiara. "I can't believe I'm just going to wander along the roadside forever. I believe that when you're thrown away, life doesn't just end there. I believe that I can be recycled and come back as another soda pop can, or a cookie sheet, or even aluminum foil!"

"Oh, no," groaned Mr. Rusty. "Another young, foolish aluminum can who believes in recycling. The roadsides are full of cans, bags, wrappers and cups like you."

Ricky tried to crunch himself lower into the tall grass. His plastic top crackled again, and the voices and sounds stopped suddenly. "Shhh!" whispered Mr. Rusty. "I heard something over there in the grass!"

"I heard it, too," said the young girl's voice.

"We hear you in there!" yelled Mr. Rusty in his deep, gruff voice. "Come out so we can see you!"

Ricky slowly pushed himself up. Mr. Rusty laughed at what he saw rising sheepishly up from the grass. The young aluminum can breathed a sigh of relief.

"Well, well," said Mr. Rusty. "Another paper cup, all dressed up with a plastic top and a plastic straw! So where did you come from, Cuppy?" he asked.

"I don't know," replied Ricky.

"It looks to me like you're from Munchin' Mike's," growled Mr. Rusty. "That's what is says on your chest!"

Ricky tried to look down, but couldn't. He only crackled. Mr. Rusty laughed hard, and the aluminum can just giggled.

"What's your name?" asked the can.

"Ricky," replied the root beer cup.

"I'm Ginger Ale-Aluminum, but you can call me Ginger." She turned to her grumpy companion. "This is Mr. Rusty."

"So, Ricky, do you believe in recycling?" asked Mr. Rusty. "Do you think that after you've been tossed out here on the roadside that there is a chance you can come back as another cup, a paper bag, a newspaper or a candy wrapper?" Mr. Rusty laughed. "That's what this eager young can believes," he said, nodding toward Ginger.

"Mr. Rusty doesn't believe in recycling," explained Ginger in a slightly scornful tone. "He thinks that once you land here on the roadside, that you stay here forever. I believe that one day I'll be picked up and eventually recycled. Then I can come back as a brand new can!"

"… or a pie tin, or aluminum foil, or a roasting pan," mocked the grumpy old rusty can. "I think it's all just a bunch of roadside trash."

Mr. Rusty talked on. "If you ask me, Cuppy — er, Ricky — I think we land here on the roadside because we're outcasts.

Our job is to stay right here and to make the roadside ugly. There's nothing more to it. That's why we're thrown here. So what do you think, huh Cup — er, Ricky?"

"Gosh, I don't know," replied Ricky. "I never really thought about it. I'm just a boy. I mean I *was* a boy!"

Mr. Rusty laughed harder than ever. "I thought Ginger here was weird with this nonsense about recycling!" he bellowed. "Now *you* come along and think we're going to believe that you were once a little *boy*!? You might as well expect me to believe that I can come back as a new bicycle!" He laughed so hard that little bits of rust flaked off of his battered old can body and fell to the ground around him.

Mr. Rusty motioned to Ricky with a rusty hand. "Come with us and meet some more litter," he said to Ricky. "You'll soon forget the idea that you were once a boy!" He tried to stop laughing, but couldn't, and more rust flakes fell around him as he chortled. Ricky, Ginger and Mr. Rusty wandered toward an opening in the tall grass farther down the road.

5. A Wild Roadside World

No one talked as they pushed through the grass toward the clearing, except for Mr. Rusty, who just mumbled. Sometimes Ricky could hear the words "recycling" and "silly" and "roadside trash" clearly through the mumbling. Ricky missed his parents and his friends, Kiara, Andrew and Keenan. He wondered where they were, and if they would be coming back this way along Green Briar Road to pick up more litter and trash. "Could this all be just a bad dream?" he thought to himself again.

As they approached the clearing, Ricky's thoughts were interrupted by sounds of more voices, gruff laughter, yelling, howling, shrill cries and all kinds of strange noises. He couldn't believe what he saw ahead. Hundreds of cans, wrappers, bottles, drink cups, and other assorted litter laughed, shouted, grunted, sputtered and hissed. It was like a giant hive full of excited and angry bees. He could hear some individual voices among the buzzing. One of the voices even reminded him of his comical Aunt Sophia, who always had a new joke to tell at every family gathering. Some pieces of litter bragged about how long they had been on the side of the road without being picked up. Some wrappers had become so old and dirty that Ricky couldn't tell whether they were candy, gum or hamburger wrappers. Ricky felt a pain inside. He felt this was an insult to his friends and the Junior Raccoons, but he knew he couldn't say a word in their defense. Ricky wondered how they could have missed all this litter on their Saturday outings.

Ricky watched in disbelief as a short, flattened cigarette butt limped up to each piece of litter in the crowd, asking "Hey, Mack, got a light?" Most of the other litter ignored the old, pitiful cigarette butt, and others just told him to go away.

Soon Ricky began to hear a new sound off in the distance. It began as a low rumbling coming from somewhere far down the road. It gradually became louder and more recognizable. Ricky had heard this sound many times before, and realized what it was just as another old can in the crowd yelled in a deep, echoing voice, "Here comes another one! Let's hope it's another Litterbug!" Ricky knew that the sound was made by a car heading in their direction, and he grew tense as the low rumbling grew into a deafening roar. The crowd of litter became more excited and began laughing, yelling and howling even louder than before. But all of the noise they made couldn't compete with the roaring, thundering sound of the approaching car, and all their commotion was soon drowned out as a big, shiny black car sped past the frenzied crowd of litter.

As the car raced by, a big brown bag full of wrappers, drink cups, cans and small boxes flew out of an open window into the fresh, clean summer air, and everything that had been inside the bag danced and sailed, spinning in the wind. The crowd of litter cheered, almost as loudly as the roaring car. Before long, everything that had been in the bag tumbled into the grass and was scattered along the roadside.

Soon another car roared by, and three aluminum cans that looked a lot like Ginger bounced into the grass on the side of the road. The crowd of litter cheered again. Ginger looked sad, but Mr. Rusty laughed his loud, gruff laugh and hobbled off to join the excitement.

Ginger turned to Ricky. "There *must* be recycling!" she exclaimed. "I don't want to be a part of this terrible world of litter!"

Deep down inside, Ricky felt ashamed. He knew how much he had loved to litter when he was a boy.

"Do you believe in recycling?" Ginger asked Ricky.

"Well… sure, I… er, I guess so," stuttered Ricky, then he paused anxiously. "Can we go somewhere else, Ginger?" he asked. "There's a playground up on the other side of the hill," said Ginger. "Except for a few candy wrappers and gum wrappers, it's pretty quiet up there. I like to go there to be alone."

"Oh, yes," said Ricky. "I've played at that… er…" Ricky caught himself and stopped in mid-sentence. He knew that Ginger would never believe him if he told her he had played there when he was a boy.

"What did you say?" asked Ginger.

"Oh, I was just saying 'yes', that I would like to go," replied Ricky nervously, but he was afraid he might meet a gum wrapper that he had thrown there when he was playing there as a boy. Then he thought that maybe the wrapper wouldn't recognize him, now that he had turned into a root beer cup from Munchin' Mike's. He wished very hard that this would be the case.

As they walked up the hill, Ricky turned to watch the laughing, yelling, howling litter. He felt sick inside when another car sped by, and more litter flew from an open window. The growing crowd of roadside litter cheered again, louder than ever. Then Ricky realized that Kiara, Andrew, Keenan, and other Junior Raccoons had probably already picked up the trash on this stretch of Green Briar Road. But thoughtless people like himself continued to litter. It would be a never-ending struggle to keep the roadside clean. Ricky was finally beginning to see why littering was so bad.

"Why don't they believe in recycling?" asked Ricky, pointing down at the cheering mob of litter.

"Oh, I think many of them do," replied Ginger. "They just don't want to admit it. They want to be thought of as tough litter that can go on and on. They want to be seen by their trash mates as invincible. If the *real* litter knew that they believed in recycling, they would be laughed off the roadside. Then they would have to find somewhere else to go. Besides that, not all litter *can* be recycled."

"What about the pieces of litter that *really* don't believe in recycling?" asked Ricky. "Or the litter that *can't* be recycled?"

"Well, I think that they were thrown on the roadside by people who really don't care about Nature or the Earth. I think those people are thoughtless and inconsiderate, and have no respect for the environment or how other people feel — people that WANT to keep the planet clean, people who don't like to see litter all over the roadsides or in parks or at the beach or…" Ginger was becoming noticeably upset, but calmed down before she continued, "I also believe that those of us who believe in recycling — those of us who believe we *will* come back in another form — were thrown here on the roadside by nice people who just don't know any better. As for the litter that can't be recycled, they could at least hope to be picked up and sent to a better place where litter can feel good about being trash — like a roadside trash barrel, or in a big plastic trash bag."

Ricky looked down and mumbled to himself, "Or in a trash can behind the garage."

Ginger glanced at Ricky. "What?" she asked. "I didn't hear you."

"Oh nothing," replied Ricky. "Really, it was nothing."

6. THE LEGEND OF THE GRIM WRAPPER

Soon Ginger and Ricky came to the top of the hill and started slowly down toward the playground. Ginger seemed to be almost in a trance, and became very quiet. Then, looking far into the distance as if she were thinking about something a thousand miles away, she said somberly, "There is one other thing you need to know."

"What is it?" asked Ricky fretfully.

Ginger went on as they continued down the hill, still looking almost as if she were in a trance. "Well, I think some of those cans and bottles and wrappers are afraid to believe in recycling. Or maybe they have lost all hope of finding their way into a trash bag or barrel or other safe place for litter."

"Why would they be afraid?" asked Ricky, feeling a little afraid now himself.

"Well, maybe they think that if they believe TOO hard they will NEVER get recycled, or even picked up and put in safe place. Maybe they think they will just stay litter forever, or they will be taken away by... by the ..." Ginger couldn't go on. She began to tremble.

"By the WHAT?" demanded Ricky, stopping in his tracks. "Taken away by the WHAT!?"

Ginger stopped, too, and turned slowly toward Ricky. In a very quiet, shaky voice — almost a whisper — she said, "Maybe they will be taken away by the *Grim Wrapper.*"

Ricky felt a chill wash over him like a bucket of ice-cold water. "Wh-wh-what's the G-G-Grim Wrapper?" he stuttered.

Ginger said nothing as she slowly turned and began walking once more toward the playground. The wind began to blow and the sky turned gray. The laughter and shouting of the litter that could be heard from the roadside faded to a creepy stillness. Another car passed, but this time there was no cheering. Ginger turned her chilling gaze once more toward Ricky, and in that same, low whisper she said, "The Grim Wrapper is litter's worst nightmare!"

"Well, what is it?! What is the Grim Wrapper?!" shouted Ricky.

"Shhhh!" Ginger looked worried. "I have never seen it, thank Goodness," she whispered, "but it is the oldest, ugliest, meanest, most evil thing that ever stalked the roadside!"

"Just the roadside?" Ricky asked hopefully.

"Well… no… it's been seen everywhere. Mr. Rusty said he saw it one gray evening just after sunset slithering slowly along the fence. Hundreds of Mr. Rusty's friends disappeared that night. Others were so horrified by what they saw that they've become stuck along the fence and may never be set free. Still others have seen it on the playground, along the bicycle path, and down along the banks of the Apple River. Laura the Lemon Drop box even saw the Grim Wrapper on the Nature Center Trail!"

"So what makes the Grim Wrapper so mean and terrible?" asked Ricky, his lid crackling.

"Once the Grim Wrapper takes you, you become litter FOREVER!" warned Ginger. "It comes mostly on days when the sky gets cloudy and dark, or at night. When the Grim Wrapper is near, the wind blows hard, and litter scatters all over the countryside."

25

Ricky looked nervously around as gray clouds continued to darken what had once been a sunny blue sky. He and Ginger watched a few lonely gum wrappers hanging tight to bending blades of tall grass and weeds, trying hard not to be pulled loose by the ever-growing wind. They hurried down to see if they could help. One of the struggling bits of litter was a little Chew-Chew Cherry gum wrapper. He cried fearfully as his grip on the bending, flailing weed began to weaken.

Thoughts on how to save this poor, frightened little wrapper raced through Ricky's mind. Suddenly an idea popped into his root beer cup head. He edged his way toward the struggling bit of cherry red paper, squeezing himself as hard as he could. Then with a loud "POP", his plastic lid opened.

"Climb inside," yelled Ricky to the frightened little wrapper, hoping to be heard above the howling wind. "You'll be safe here!"

In one quick motion, the frail Chew-Chew Cherry gum wrapper let go of the now nearly uprooted weed and grabbed the edge of the root beer cup that was Ricky. After he climbed safely inside, Ginger pushed Ricky's lid back on with a crackly "KA-POP."

Ricky heard a faint little voice coming from inside him. "Oh, it's icy cold in here. I'm getting all wet! But I love the smell of root beer." Ginger and Ricky giggled nervously.

"What's your name?" asked Ginger, leaning toward Ricky so she could hear the faint voice inside Ricky.

"Jerry" came the timid reply.

"I'm Ginger. And you're inside Ricky."

Ricky thought it strange to hear a little voice inside him that wasn't his. "Hi Ginger, hi Ricky," said Jerry. "Nice to meet you both."

The sky continued to darken, and the wind howled like a prowling wolf. Ricky looked at Ginger, who turned back and stared out onto the playground. "We must leave here now!" she yelled back to Ricky and Jerry, hoping they could hear her over the wailing wind.

They struggled back up the hill away from the playground. When they got to the top, they could see the litter below bouncing and tumbling in the wind. Some rolled across the road to the other side. Some were pulled from the grass and carried out of sight in an instant. The crowd of litter was being scattered all along both sides of the road, and all was quiet except for the howling wind.

Ricky felt afraid. He wished hard that he would turn back into a boy, but nothing happened.

Now he was afraid that he would become litter FOREVER!

"What's going on?" asked Jerry in a shaky little voice, still hiding safely inside Ricky. Ricky did not answer. He himself did not know what was happening.

7. A Horrible, Horrible Sight

Suddenly the wind died and all the litter lay still. The sudden silence was almost more frightening than the sound of the wind. Ginger barked to Ricky, "Let's head for the tall grass further down, and hurry! But whatever you do, don't get too close to the road!"

When they got to the tall grass, Ginger signaled to get down low. Ricky scrunched down as low as he could go. The little Chew-Chew Cherry gum wrapper twitched nervously inside him. "Wh... Where are we? I want my Mommy!" cried Jerry.

"Shhhh!!" whispered Ginger. "Your mother may be one of the lucky ones. She's probably been picked up and is in a cozy trash bag somewhere waiting for you." No one said another word. They all just waited in the tall, still grass.

Then Ricky heard a strange sound from afar. He knew it wasn't another car. He could tell it wasn't the wind. It was something else. It was a sound he had never ever heard before. He looked hard at Ginger, hoping she would smile and tell him it was nothing, that everything would be okay. But instead, her aluminum can eyes opened wide in fear. She moved her mouth slowly, barely able to whisper the two terrifying words, "G-G-G-Grim Wr-Wr-Wr-*Wrapper*!"

Ricky nearly froze with fear. Even the water inside him felt like it was turning back into ice. He heard Jerry sigh nervously, almost crying. The strange sound grew louder and closer. It was a crackling, crunching, oozing, scratchy, drippy sound. It was like all the litter of every kind from every roadside, every playground, and every sidewalk had been lumped together into the biggest, ugliest, stinkiest glob of litter in the whole wide world.

The slimy, slippery, stinky thing that litter everywhere feared as the Grim Wrapper slithered closer and closer. Suddenly Ricky felt something inside near his plastic top. The little gum wrapper was trying to push Ricky's plastic lid open. Ricky squeezed tight, trying to keep his lid on when he heard a loud "POP!" Much to his dismay, the lid opened, and the little Chew-Chew Cherry gum wrapper peeked out to see what was making this awful sound.

"Get down, Jerry!" yelled Ricky. But it was too late. If the Grim Wrapper had not seen Jerry peeking out, it had surely heard Ricky yell. The slithery, slimy, crackly, crunchy sound suddenly stopped. Ricky rose slowly to see what was happening. Little Jerry stared out in fear. The Grim Wrapper stood just a few feet away. It was a horrible, horrible sight. It was dirty and crumpled and slimy and gooey and smelled worse than anything in the whole wide world. Pieces of every kind of litter from everywhere on the planet Earth were globbed together. A cluster of tiny sinister red, yellow and green eyes — probably the remnants of some discarded toys or electronic devices —blinked out of unison from within the foul-smelling, frightening, oozing mass. Newer litter had already been taken by the Grim Wrapper. Ricky recognized a few cleaner scraps of paper stuck to the dark, dingy cloak of the dirty, rotten, stinky glob of evil called the Grim Wrapper. Ricky felt sick.

Suddenly, Ricky heard Jerry utter a frightful squeak. Ricky could feel him being sucked out. With a "WHISSHHH", the little wrapper was gone. In the blink of an eye, the poor little Chew-Chew Cherry gum wrapper named Jerry was stuck to the cloak of this horrible beast made of litter.

Without thinking, Ricky lunged through the tall grass toward the Grim Wrapper. He wanted to save poor little Jerry, who just seconds before had been hiding safely inside him.

Ricky felt a tugging at his straw. Ginger had grabbed on to him by the tip of his straw, trying to hold him back. But Ricky was determined to save little Jerry. He let his straw slip out through the top of his lid, and Ginger stood in shock, straw in hand, as Ricky bolted toward the Grim Wrapper.

Ricky stopped in his tracks at what he saw before him. Poor little Jerry was not the only victim to be claimed by the Grim Wrapper. There, stuck among the garbage and goo, was poor Mr. Rusty. He could barely move his hand as he waved sadly to Ricky and muttered a few last words. "Ya see, Cuppy, I told you how it would end!" He paused for a moment, his breathing strained, and the words came slowly and with much difficulty. "Be sure to tell that sweet little Ginger… that I hope, for her sake… and the sake of *all* litter that believes in recycling… that recycling is… is a *reality*… Well… I… I guess this is 'good-bye', Cup… er… I mean… Ricky." Mr. Rusty could not say another word as he fell under the evil spell of the Grim Wrapper.

Ginger rushed back to Ricky's side. The strange, terrible force of the Grim Wrapper had begun to pull them both closer and closer. It was like being sucked into a powerful tornado. Ricky grabbed Ginger's hand.

"Don't let go!" cried Ginger.

"Never!" answered Ricky. He was more frightened than he had ever been in his whole life. He looked at Ginger as they were pulled closer toward the ugly, horrible, stinking glob of garbage and goo, and he saw the fear in her eyes, too.

"Remember, Ricky," she said calmly, in spite of her fear, "we will come back. We will be recycled, but you must believe it to be true!"

Ricky knew it would be only seconds before the Grim Wrapper sucked them in. He gazed into Ginger's eyes. "I *do* believe in recycling. I really, *really* do believe in recycling!"

8. A Root Beer Cup No More

Just then, Ricky heard familiar voices that didn't belong to Ginger, or Jerry, or Mr. Rusty. The voices came from above. Ricky looked up to see three towering giants moving toward him, Ginger and the Grim Wrapper. He couldn't believe what he was seeing! The three giants were his friends and Junior Raccoons, Kiara, Andrew and Keenan. They each had a big plastic bag in hand and were picking up roadside litter. Ricky called out in desperation. "Kiara! Keenan! Andrew! Do you hear me?! It's me, Ricky!"

Suddenly there was a loud "PFOOOOFFF", a blinding flash of light, and a swirling wind. The light was the brightest Ricky had ever seen. Well, almost the brightest. Ricky thought for sure this meant that it was too late to be saved, that he and Ginger would be sucked into the evil world of garbage and litter that was ruled by the Grim Wrapper.

But the wind died, the light slowly faded, and all was quiet again. To his surprise, Ricky found himself sitting on the side of the road, staring up at his friends, Kiara, Andrew and Keenan. They no longer looked like giants. When he moved his head up and down, he no longer heard the crackling sound that had once been a part of his every movement.

Kiara was startled and looked down. "Where did *you* come from?!" she cried, and turned and grabbed Keenan by the arm while Andrew stood, open-mouthed, in disbelief.

"Owwww!" yelled Keenan. "That really hurts! It's only Ricky!"

"Yes, I *know* it's only Ricky!" replied Kiara. "But where did he come from?"

"I don't know," said Keenan. He too was puzzled by the sudden appearance of Ricky. "Where *did* you come from, Ricky?" Andrew continued to stare, still dumb-founded by the sudden appearance of Ricky.

"I … er, I saw you all from across the road," said Ricky, hoping they would believe him. "I ran over when I saw you weren't looking! I just wanted to play a trick on you guys!" Kiara and Keenan looked at each other in disbelief. They wanted very much to believe Ricky, but were still very suspicious.

Ricky quickly changed the subject, hoping to draw his friends' thoughts away from his mysterious and sudden appearance there on the side of Green Briar Road. "You know," said Ricky calmly. "I've changed my mind about helping you guys pick up litter along the roadside. I want to help you today, right now. I'll help you every single day, if I have to!"

Ricky stood up and looked down where he had been sitting. There at his feet was a shiny aluminum can that said "Ginger Ale" diagonally across the can in flowery, cursive letters. Ricky picked it up and stared at it intently. He smiled and said, "Ginger was right. Now I really *do* believe in recycling. Everyone should believe in recycling!" He held the Ginger Ale can up in front of him, and as if talking directly to the can, said softly "I knew all along we would escape the Grim Wrapper!"

Kiara, Andrew and Keenan all exchanged bewildered looks, now even more puzzled by Ricky's behavior. Just then, the gray clouds began to break up. The sun smiled a warm, bright yellow smile of sunlight. In the distance, Ricky could hear the sound of a car approaching. Something inside him made him afraid that someone would throw another bag of trash out the window as the car sped by. But as Ricky and his friends turned to see the oncoming car, they all smiled. Ricky jumped with joy as he recognized the car to be that of his parents, his mother and father beaming smiles from the front seat. The car slowed to the side of the road, and Ricky ran as fast as he could to greet his parents.

The passenger side door flew open, and Ricky's father jumped from the car. "Where on Earth have you been?!" he exclaimed, clearly worried about his son. Ricky hugged his father tighter than ever before, then ran around to the driver's side of the car to meet his mother as she leapt from behind the steering wheel. She wrapped her arms lovingly around Ricky and gave him a huge hug, almost squeezing the breath out of him.

"Your mother and I are so sorry for having left you at the roadside picnic table," said his father. "We were absolutely certain you had gotten into the car with us!"

Ricky began to reply, "Oh, you didn't leave me…" but stopped, knowing the truth would be totally unbelievable. "Oh, that's okay," said Ricky, quickly changing his tone. "Besides, I met Kiara, Andrew and Keenan as I started walking in the direction of home. I've decided to help them clean up the litter along Green Briar Road. And you know what, Mom and Dad?"

"What, Ricky?" replied his parents at exactly the same time.

"I'm never going to litter again — EVER! And I'm going to start recycling right NOW!"

"That's wonderful news!" laughed his mother.

Ricky's father smiled at Kiara, Andrew and Keenan. "I want to thank you for helping Ricky to change his ways. I don't know what you said to him to convince him to stop littering, but whatever it was, it worked." The three friends looked at each other and shrugged their shoulders.

"We didn't say…" began Andrew, but stopped suddenly when Kiara nudged him in the side. "I mean, you're very welcome, sir".

"Ricky, I know you'd like to help your friends more, but let's go home and have some dinner first," said Ricky's father. They all said goodbye to the three Junior Raccoons, and asked them if they would like a ride home. They all politely refused, saying they wanted to pick up some more litter. As Ricky and his parents climbed back into the car, he turned for one last look at the roadside. "I'll be back to help you," he said to his friends. "I *promise*!" Then they drove off toward home.

"You know," said Kiara, "sometimes Ricky can be kind of weird. But I'm glad he's going to help us."

"Me too," replied Andrew and Keenan at the same time. "I just hope he doesn't talk to *all* the cans!"

They all laughed as they walked slowly along the roadside, picking up litter as they went, chatting with each other about how they would separate the recycling once they got home.

Made in the USA
Las Vegas, NV
09 December 2021

36748940R00026